This book belongs to

....

The Monkey & the Crocodile

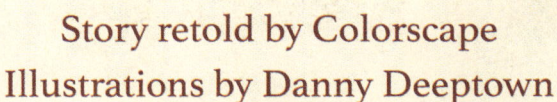

Story retold by Colorscape
Illustrations by Danny Deeptown

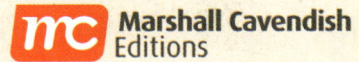

Once upon a time, there was a monkey who lived in an apple tree by the edge of a large lagoon. The tree provided the monkey with juicy red apples, shelter from the rain and shade from the sun.

One day, a hungry crocodile swam up to the bank. He noticed the monkey in the tree. "Dear monkey, I am so hungry. Do you have any food that you can share with me?"

The monkey was startled as he knew the crocodile could eat him in one gulp. But he put aside his fears and said, "This tree has lots of delicious apples. Would you like to try some?"

"Yes," the crocodile replied and opened his jaws, showing all his teeth.
The monkey calmly threw a few apples down.

"These are delicious! Thank you so much," said the crocodile happily.
Then he slipped back into the river and swam home.

At sunrise the next morning, the crocodile returned.
"Those apples were scrumptious. May I have some more please?"
"Of course," replied the monkey. "There is plenty to go around."
"You're too kind," said the crocodile.

From that day on, the crocodile would visit the monkey every day.
Besides filling their bellies with apples, they would share wonderful stories
about the lagoon, and laugh and joke between themselves.

As the days passed, their friendship grew.

One day, the monkey asked where the crocodile lived.

"I live on an island in the middle of the lagoon with my family. Speaking of which, it's getting late and I should get going."

"See you tomorrow, my friend," said the monkey.

"See you soon," said the crocodile as he disappeared under the surface of the water.

    Back on his island, the crocodile's family asked him where he went every day.

    "I visit my friend, the monkey, on the lagoon's edge. We chat and eat apples all day."

    With their mouths watering, the other crocodiles said,
"You mean there's a monkey that's been fed on apples, living across the lagoon?"

"Yes," replied the crocodile. "The apples are so juicy and sweet."
The others exclaimed, "But imagine how sweet the monkey would taste!"
"Wait... what? You can't eat the monkey. He's my best friend!" said the crocodile.
"But we're your family. And we're hungry. Why don't you go and bring your friend here?"

The crocodile was sad, but he went to meet the monkey as usual the next day. The monkey was waiting happily for his friend. He had prepared a pile of freshly-picked apples to share. But he sensed something was wrong.

"What's wrong, my dear friend?" asked the monkey.

"My family would like to invite you to our island. They say I should return your hospitality."

The monkey was wary and asked if there was anything the crocodile needed to tell him. The crocodile shook his head in silence.

"How will I get to the island?" the monkey asked.
"You can sit on my back and I will carry you there," said the crocodile.
The monkey agreed but sensed that something was wrong.

"Is everything okay?" asked the monkey as the crocodile glided across the lagoon.

"Um, yes, everything is fine. I just can't wait for you to meet my family."

"OH NO!" exclaimed the monkey suddenly.

"What's wrong?" cried the crocodile as he came to a stop.

"Apples! I wanted to bring some as a gift for your family!" exclaimed the monkey.

"There's no need for a gift. It's just you they want... er, want to see!" the crocodile blurted out.

And without warning, he dove into the water.
The monkey held on and yelled, "Please!
How could I visit my best friend's family without bringing a gift?"

"Very well," said the crocodile.
He swam back up to the surface and headed for the apple tree.

The journey back was a long and awkward one for the monkey. And as soon as he could, he leapt off the crocodile's back and scrambled up the apple tree.

When he was at the top, the monkey shouted down, "Crocodile, we were friends, but you were taking me to be dinner for your family!"

The crocodile admitted that he had not been a good friend to the kind monkey.

"I am very sorry," he bawled.

The monkey watched the crocodile drift sadly away. He was sad too, but felt relieved to be alive. He sat back, picked a juicy apple and resumed his life as before.

Once upon a time, there was a monkey who lived in an apple tree by the edge of a large lagoon. The tree provided the monkey with juicy red apples, shelter from the rain and shade from the sun.

One day, a hungry crocodile swam up to the bank. He noticed the monkey in the tree. "Dear monkey, I am so hungry. Do you have any food that you can share with me?"

The monkey was startled as he knew the crocodile could eat him in one gulp. But he put aside his fears and said, "This tree has lots of delicious apples. Would you like to try some?"

"Yes," the crocodile replied and opened his jaws, showing all his teeth.
The monkey calmly threw a few apples down.

"These are delicious! Thank you so much," said the crocodile happily.
Then he slipped back into the river and swam home.

At sunrise the next morning, the crocodile returned.

"Those apples were scrumptious. May I have some more please?"

"Of course," replied the monkey. "There is plenty to go around."

"You're too kind," said the crocodile.

From that day on, the crocodile would visit the monkey every day. Besides filling their bellies with apples, they would share wonderful stories about the lagoon, and laugh and joke between themselves.

As the days passed, their friendship grew.

One day, the monkey asked where the crocodile lived.

"I live on an island in the middle of the lagoon with my family. Speaking of which, it's getting late and I should get going."

"See you tomorrow, my friend," said the monkey.

"See you soon," said the crocodile as he disappeared under the surface of the water.

Back on his island, the crocodile's family asked him where he went every day.

"I visit my friend, the monkey, on the lagoon's edge. We chat and eat apples all day."

With their mouths watering, the other crocodiles said,
"You mean there's a monkey that's been fed on apples, living across the lagoon?"

"Yes," replied the crocodile. "The apples are so juicy and sweet."

The others exclaimed, "But imagine how sweet the monkey would taste!"

"Wait... what? You can't eat the monkey. He's my best friend!" said the crocodile.

"But we're your family. And we're hungry. Why don't you go and bring your friend here?"

The crocodile was sad, but he went to meet the monkey as usual the next day.
The monkey was waiting happily for his friend. He had prepared a pile of
freshly-picked apples to share. But he sensed something was wrong.

"What's wrong, my dear friend?" asked the monkey.

"My family would like to invite you to our island. They say I should return your hospitality."

The monkey was wary and asked if there was anything the crocodile needed to tell him. The crocodile shook his head in silence.

"How will I get to the island?" the monkey asked.

"You can sit on my back and I will carry you there," said the crocodile.

The monkey agreed but sensed that something was wrong.

"Is everything okay?" asked the monkey as the crocodile glided across the lagoon.

"Um, yes, everything is fine. I just can't wait for you to meet my family."

"OH NO!" exclaimed the monkey suddenly.

"What's wrong?" cried the crocodile as he came to a stop.

"Apples! I wanted to bring some as a gift for your family!" exclaimed the monkey.

"There's no need for a gift. It's just you they want… er, want to see!" the crocodile blurted out.

And without warning, he dove into the water.

The monkey held on and yelled, "Please!
How could I visit my best friend's family without bringing a gift?"

"Very well," said the crocodile.
He swam back up to the surface and headed for the apple tree.

The journey back was a long and awkward one for the monkey. And as soon as he could, he leapt off the crocodile's back and scrambled up the apple tree.

When he was at the top, the monkey shouted down, "Crocodile, we were friends, but you were taking me to be dinner for your family!"

The crocodile admitted that he had not been a good friend to the kind monkey.

"I am very sorry," he bawled.

The monkey watched the crocodile drift sadly away. He was sad too, but felt relieved to be alive. He sat back, picked a juicy apple and resumed his life as before.

The Monkey & the Crocodile
ISBN 978 981 5169 20 1

© 2022 Colorscape
Illustrations © 2022 Danny Deeptown

This edition published in 2024 by Marshall Cavendish International (Asia) Pte Ltd

Published by Marshall Cavendish Editions
An imprint of Marshall Cavendish International

All rights reserved

No part of this publication may be reproduced, stored in a retrieval system or transmitted, in any form or by any means, electronic, mechanical, photocopying, recording or otherwise, without the prior permission of the copyright owner. Requests for permission should be addressed to the Publisher, Marshall Cavendish International (Asia) Private Limited, 1 New Industrial Road, Singapore 536196. Tel: (65) 6213 9300 E-mail: genref@sg.marshallcavendish.com Website: www.marshallcavendish.com

The publisher makes no representation or warranties with respect to the contents of this book, and specifically disclaims any implied warranties or merchantability or fitness for any particular purpose, and shall in no event be liable for any loss of profit or any other commercial damage, including but not limited to special, incidental, consequential, or other damages.

Other Marshall Cavendish Offices:
Marshall Cavendish Corporation, 800 Westchester Ave, Suite N-641, Rye Brook, NY 10573, USA • Marshall Cavendish International (Thailand) Co Ltd, 253 Asoke, 16th Floor, Sukhumvit 21 Road, Klongtoey Nua, Wattana, Bangkok 10110, Thailand • Marshall Cavendish (Malaysia) Sdn Bhd, Times Subang, Lot 46, Subang Hi-Tech Industrial Park, Batu Tiga, 40000 Shah Alam, Selangor Darul Ehsan, Malaysia

Marshall Cavendish is a registered trademark of Times Publishing Limited

Printed in Singapore